BURIED MOON

BURIED MOON

Retold by MARGARET HODGES

Illustrated by
JAMICHAEL HENTERLY

Little, Brown and Company
Boston   Toronto   London

First Edition

This story was first collected by folklorist Marie Clothilde
Balfour, who heard it told by a nine-year-old girl. It appeared
in Mrs. Balfour's article "Legends of the Cars" for the British
publication *Folk-Lore*, Vol. II, No. II, June 1891.

Library of Congress Cataloging-in-Publication Data
Hodges, Margaret.
Buried Moon / retold by Margaret Hodges; illustrated by Jamichael
Henterly.
    p.   cm.
    Summary: Who will rescue the Moon after she is buried in a dark
pool by witches, goblins, and other evil creatures who have always
resented her bright, shining light?
    ISBN 0-316-36793-1
    [1. Folklore. 2. Moon — Folklore.]   I. Henterly, Jamichael, ill.
II. Title.
PZ8.1.H69Bu   1990   89-2664
[E] — dc20   CIP
                                                              AC
10 9 8 7 6 5 4 3 2 1

WOR

Published simultaneously in Canada
by Little, Brown & Company (Canada) Limited

Printed in the United States of America

To Katharine Briggs

M. H.

For Skye Juniper

J. H.

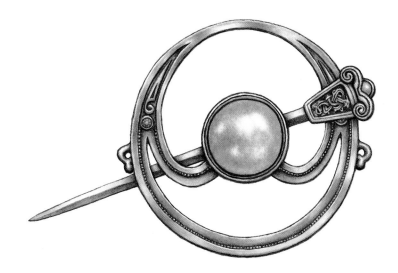

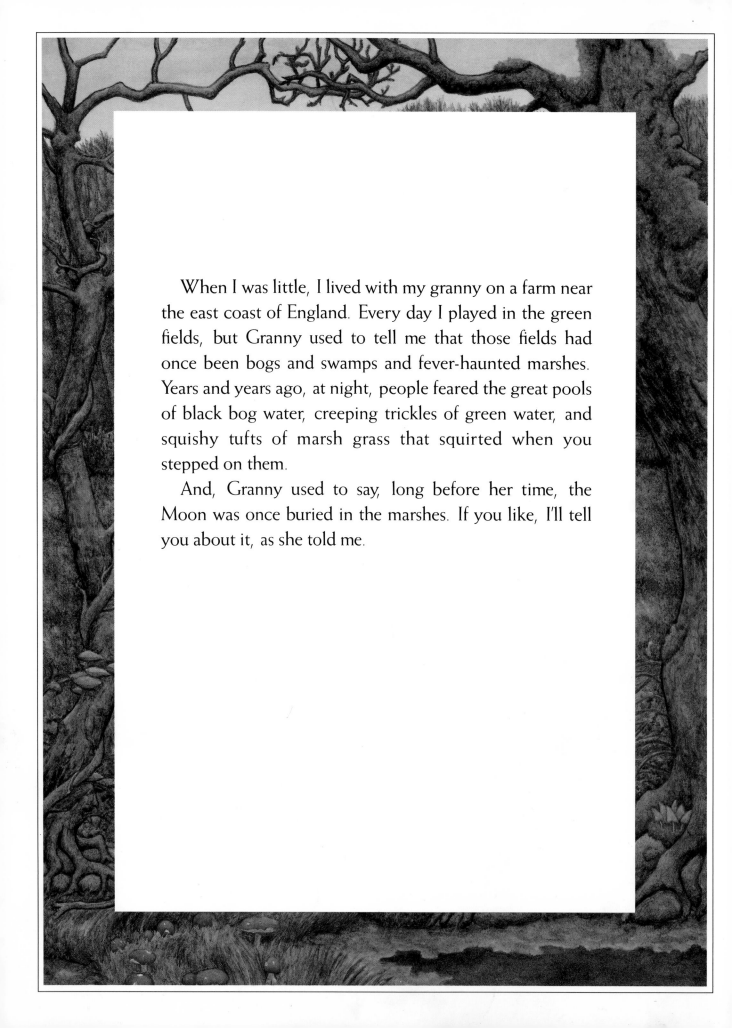

When I was little, I lived with my granny on a farm near the east coast of England. Every day I played in the green fields, but Granny used to tell me that those fields had once been bogs and swamps and fever-haunted marshes. Years and years ago, at night, people feared the great pools of black bog water, creeping trickles of green water, and squishy tufts of marsh grass that squirted when you stepped on them.

And, Granny used to say, long before her time, the Moon was once buried in the marshes. If you like, I'll tell you about it, as she told me.

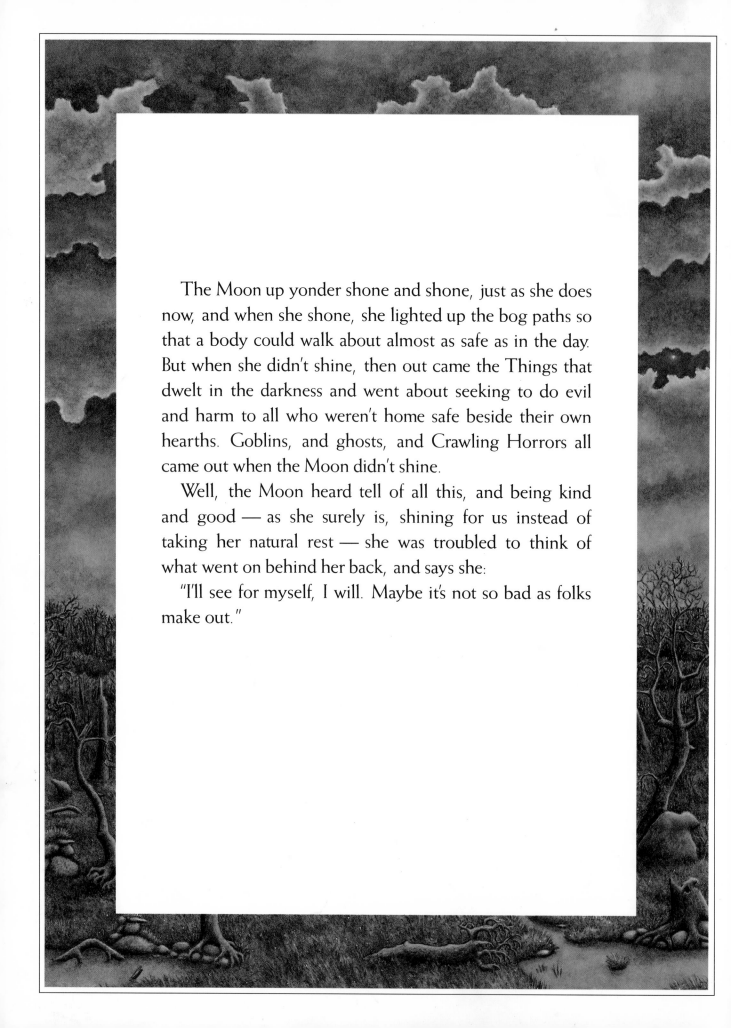

The Moon up yonder shone and shone, just as she does now, and when she shone, she lighted up the bog paths so that a body could walk about almost as safe as in the day. But when she didn't shine, then out came the Things that dwelt in the darkness and went about seeking to do evil and harm to all who weren't home safe beside their own hearths. Goblins, and ghosts, and Crawling Horrors all came out when the Moon didn't shine.

Well, the Moon heard tell of all this, and being kind and good — as she surely is, shining for us instead of taking her natural rest — she was troubled to think of what went on behind her back, and says she:

"I'll see for myself, I will. Maybe it's not so bad as folks make out."

Sure enough, at the month's end, down she stepped, wrapped up in a black cloak with a black hood over her yellow, shining hair. Straight she went to the bog edge and looked about. Water here and water there, waving tufts of grass, and trembling earth, and great black snags of trees, all twisted and bent. Before her, all was dark — all dark but the glimmer of the stars in the pools and the light that came from her own white feet, stealing out of her black cloak.

On she went into the midst of the bogs, and it was a queer sight she saw. Witches grinned as they rode past on their great black cats, the Evil Eye glowered from the darkest corners, and the will-o'-the-wisps danced about with lanterns swinging on their backs.

The Moon drew her cloak closer about her and trembled, but she wouldn't go back without seeing all there was to be seen. So on she went, stepping as light as the wind in summer from tuft to tuft between the greedy gurgling water holes. Just as she came near a big black pool, her foot slipped, and she would have tumbled in if she had not grabbed a nearby snag to steady herself. But as soon as she touched it, it twined itself around her wrists like a pair of handcuffs. She pulled and twisted and fought to get free, but it did no good. She was caught fast.

She looked about and wondered if help would come by, but she saw only shifting, flurrying Evil Things coming and going here and there.

Presently, as she stood trembling in the dark, she heard something in the distance — a voice that called and called till the marshes were full of the pitiful crying. And then she heard steps floundering along, squishing in the mud and slipping on the tufts, and through the darkness she saw hands catching at the snags, and a pale face with great scared eyes.

It was a man astray in the bogs, and around him the grinning goblins and the Creeping Horrors crawled and crowded, and the will-o'-the-wisps shook with evil glee as they led him farther and farther from the right track. Dazed with fear, he struggled toward their flickering lights that looked like help and safety. And when the poor Moon saw that he was getting nearer to the deep holes and farther from the path, she was so sorry for him that she struggled harder than ever. And though she couldn't get loose, she twisted and turned till her hood fell back off her shining yellow hair, and the beautiful light that came from it drove away the darkness.

Oh, the man cried with joy to see the light again! At once the Evil Things fled back into the dark corners, for they cannot bear the light. And the man could see where he was, and where the path was, and how to get out of the marsh. He was in such haste to get away from the ghosts and goblins that he scarcely looked at the brightness that came from the beautiful, shining yellow hair, streaming out over the black cloak and falling to the water at his feet. And the Moon herself was so taken up with saving him that she clean forgot she needed help herself.

So off he went, sobbing with joy, flying for his life out of the terrible bogs. The Moon, wanting to go with him, pulled and fought till she fell on her knees at the foot of the snag. And as she lay there, gasping for breath, the black hood fell forward over her head again. She tried to throw it back, but it was caught in her hair and wouldn't go. So out went the blessed light, and back came the darkness with all its Evil Things. They came crowding round her, shrieking with rage and spite, for they knew their old enemy, the bright shining Moon.

"Drat thee!" yelled the witches. "Thou has spoiled our spells all these past years!"

"And sent us to brood in the corners!" howled the goblins.

"Smother her! Smother her!" whispered the Crawling Horrors, and they twined themselves round her knees.

And the poor Moon crouched down and wished she were dead and done with.

Then a pale light began to come in the sky, and it drew near the dawning. When the Evil Things saw that, they feared they shouldn't have time to work their will, and they caught hold of her with horrid long fingers and pushed her deep in the water at the foot of the snag. The goblins fetched a strange big stone and rolled it on top of her to keep her from rising. They told two will-o'-the-wisps to take turns watching on the black snag to see that she lay safe and still and couldn't get out to help the poor bog folk at night.

And so there lay the Moon, buried in the bog till someone would set her loose. But who'd know where to look for her?

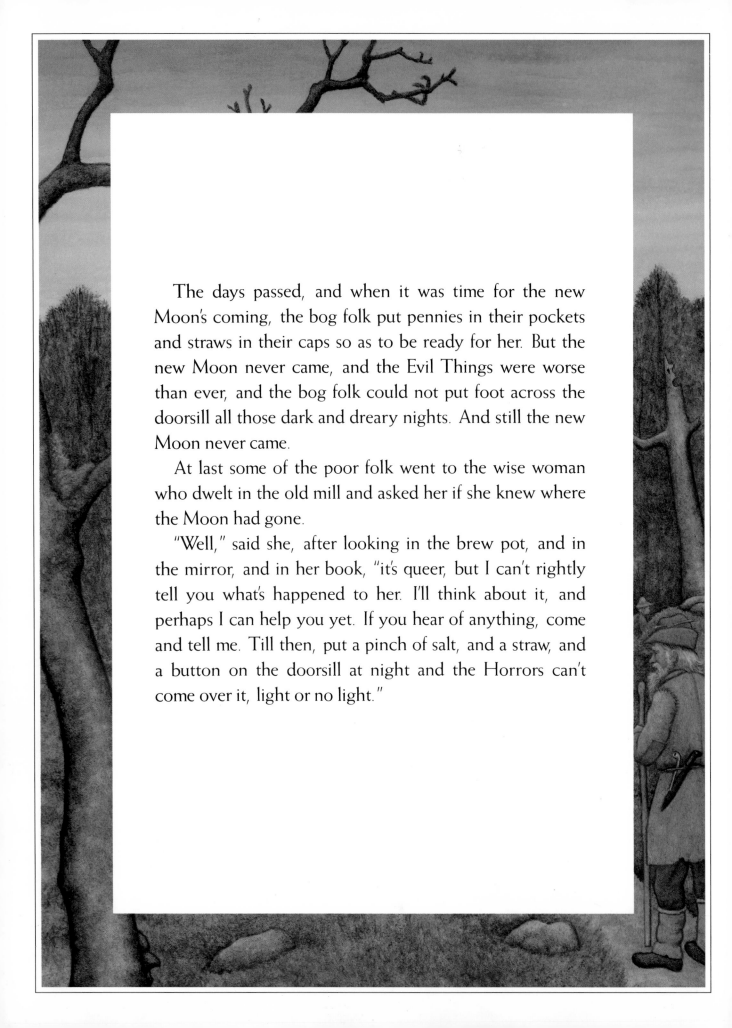

The days passed, and when it was time for the new Moon's coming, the bog folk put pennies in their pockets and straws in their caps so as to be ready for her. But the new Moon never came, and the Evil Things were worse than ever, and the bog folk could not put foot across the doorsill all those dark and dreary nights. And still the new Moon never came.

At last some of the poor folk went to the wise woman who dwelt in the old mill and asked her if she knew where the Moon had gone.

"Well," said she, after looking in the brew pot, and in the mirror, and in her book, "it's queer, but I can't rightly tell you what's happened to her. I'll think about it, and perhaps I can help you yet. If you hear of anything, come and tell me. Till then, put a pinch of salt, and a straw, and a button on the doorsill at night and the Horrors can't come over it, light or no light."

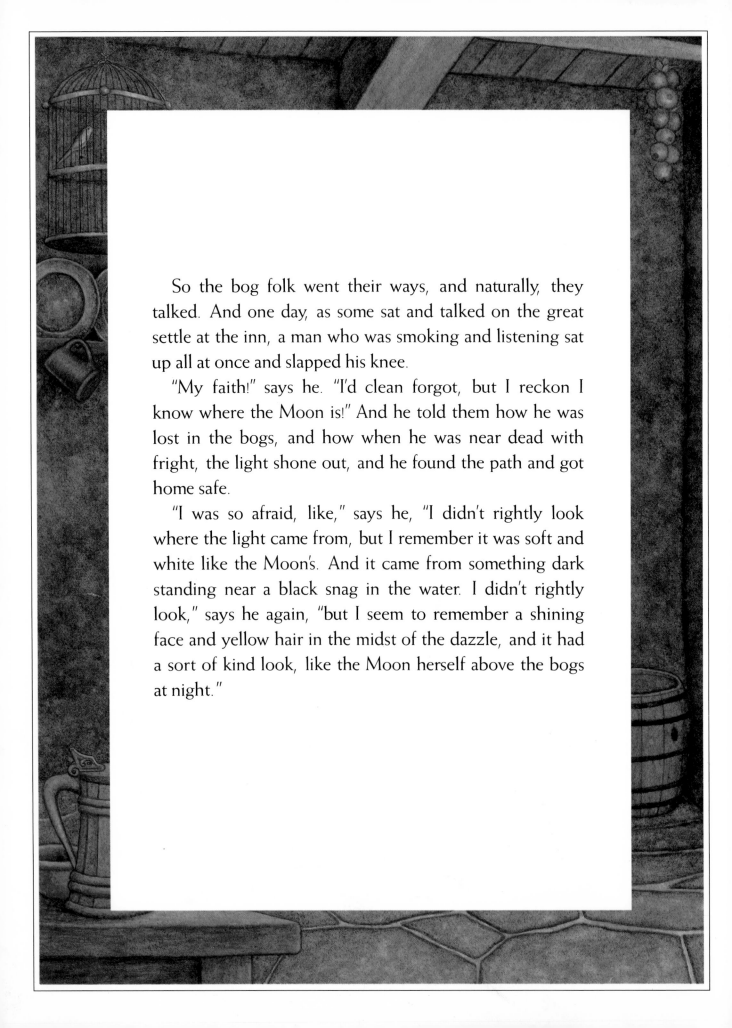

So the bog folk went their ways, and naturally, they talked. And one day, as some sat and talked on the great settle at the inn, a man who was smoking and listening sat up all at once and slapped his knee.

"My faith!" says he. "I'd clean forgot, but I reckon I know where the Moon is!" And he told them how he was lost in the bogs, and how when he was near dead with fright, the light shone out, and he found the path and got home safe.

"I was so afraid, like," says he, "I didn't rightly look where the light came from, but I remember it was soft and white like the Moon's. And it came from something dark standing near a black snag in the water. I didn't rightly look," says he again, "but I seem to remember a shining face and yellow hair in the midst of the dazzle, and it had a sort of kind look, like the Moon herself above the bogs at night."

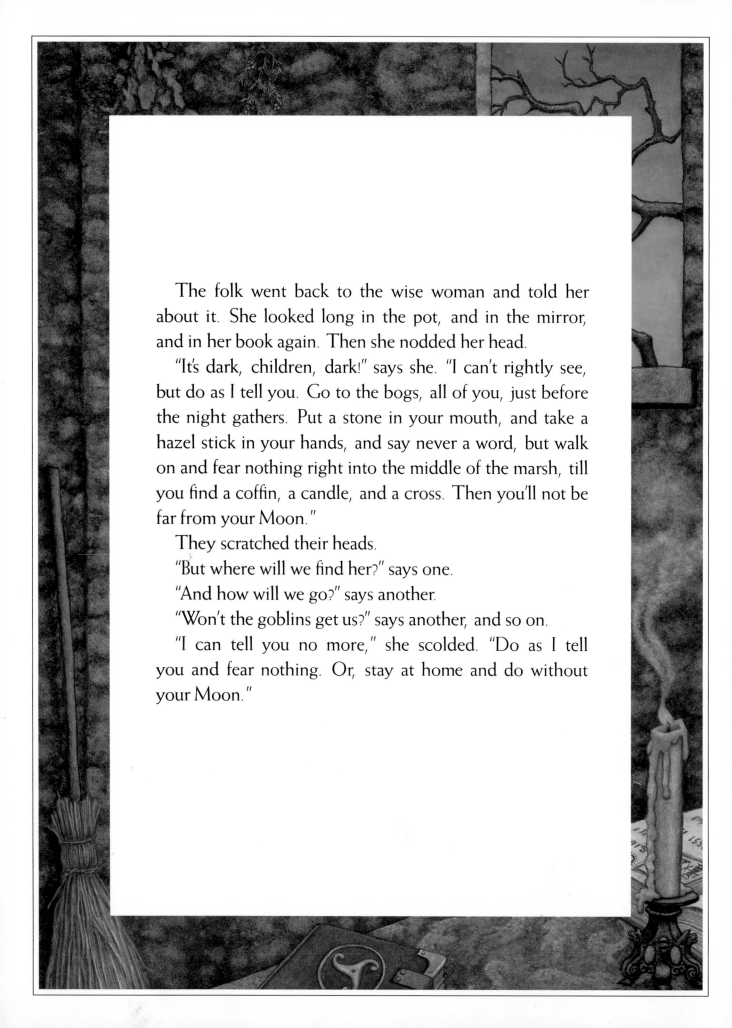

The folk went back to the wise woman and told her about it. She looked long in the pot, and in the mirror, and in her book again. Then she nodded her head.

"It's dark, children, dark!" says she. "I can't rightly see, but do as I tell you. Go to the bogs, all of you, just before the night gathers. Put a stone in your mouth, and take a hazel stick in your hands, and say never a word, but walk on and fear nothing right into the middle of the marsh, till you find a coffin, a candle, and a cross. Then you'll not be far from your Moon."

They scratched their heads.

"But where will we find her?" says one.

"And how will we go?" says another.

"Won't the goblins get us?" says another, and so on.

"I can tell you no more," she scolded. "Do as I tell you and fear nothing. Or, stay at home and do without your Moon."

The next night, in the darkling, out they went together, every man with a stone in his mouth and a hazel stick in his hand, and feeling, you can guess, afraid and creepy. They stumbled and staggered along the paths into the midst of the bogs and saw nothing, though they heard sighings and flutterings and felt cold wet fingers touching them. But on they went, looking around for the coffin, the candle, and the cross, till they came near to the pool beside the great snag, where the Moon lay buried. And all at once they stopped, shaking with fear, for there was the great stone, half in and half out of the water, looking for all the world like a strange big coffin. And at the head was the black snag, stretching out its arms in a dark, gruesome cross, and on it a tiny light flickered like a dying candle. And they knelt down in the mud and prayed, but without speaking, for they knew the Evil Things would catch them if they didn't do as the wise woman had told them.

Then they went nearer, took hold of the big stone, and shoved it up. And afterward they said that for one tiny minute they saw a strange and beautiful face looking up at them, glad like, out of the black water. But then the light came so quick and so shining that they stepped back, dazed by it and by the great angry wail that came from the fleeing Horrors.

And the very next minute, when they could see again, there was the full Moon in the sky, bright and beautiful and kind as ever, smiling down at them and making the bogs and the paths as clear as day — stealing into the very corners, as though she'd have driven the darkness and the goblins clean away, if she could.

So home the bog folk went, with light hearts, and ever since, the Moon shines brighter and clearer over the bogs than anywhere else, for she remembers that the bog folk sought her and found her when she was buried in the bog.

And mark my words, it is all true, for my granny has seen the snag with its two arms, for all the world like a great cross, and the green, slimy water at its foot, where the poor Moon was buried, and the stone nearby that kept her down before the wise woman sent the bog folk to set her free and put her in the sky again.